Lupé

A Wolf Pup's First Year

WALRUS
BOOKS

Story by Rebecca L. Grambo Photography by Daniel J. Cox

Yellowstone National Park lies cradled in the Rocky Mountains of Wyoming and Montana. It is the world's oldest national park and one of the largest in the United States. It was set aside by President Ulysses S. Grant in 1872 to protect the land and animals for all to enjoy.

On a chilly April day, deep within the park, a pack of wolves traveled a familiar path. As the wolves trotted along, they lifted their noses often to catch whatever scents might be on the breeze. Aspen, the top female in the pack, and her partner, Teton, had mated in February. Now Aspen was pregnant and would soon need a safe, sheltered place to give birth to her pups.

Aspen was heading for the den site she had used last year. It lay at the heart of the pack's territory, away from roads and people. The den entrance was on a slope that faced south so it would warm up quickly in the spring sun. From the outside, no one would guess that the hole in the ground led through a tunnel into a room big enough for a mother wolf to lie with her pups. A nearby stream was handy when the wolves wanted a drink.

"This is a good place," Aspen thought as she wriggled out of the entrance after checking the den. "If I dig it out a bit to get rid of the mess left from last year, I will be all ready for my pups to be born."

Teton sniffed inside the den and then turned to nuzzle Aspen. The other wolves in the pack—Sinter, Sage, and Lily—had settled down for a short nap. With a yawn, Teton lay down, and after one more look at the den, Aspen did, too. For a while, she watched fat snowflakes drifting lazily down from the gray sky. Then she tucked her nose deeper into her tail, closed her eyes, and slept.

For three days, Aspen had been restless. She stayed close to the den and wouldn't let Teton come inside with her. Finally, it was time. Aspen lay inside the chamber at the back of the den while the other wolves crowded together outside the entrance, whining excitedly.

As each pup was born, the first thing it felt was its mother's soft tongue licking it clean and clearing its nose so it could breathe. Then Aspen bit through the umbilical cord that had fed the pup while it was inside her. She nudged the pup toward her stomach. The pup could not see or hear, but instinct helped it to find a nipple and begin to suckle.

Aspen lifted her head to look at her pups. They were so small and helpless, these three little creatures: each weighed only about half a kilogram (a pound). With damp fur and bellies full of milk, the pups snuggled into Aspen's soft coat. They needed her body heat to keep them warm. She would remain with them almost constantly at first, nursing them four or five times a day. The other pack members would bring Aspen food until she could leave the pups alone for a little while. Aspen lowered her head and gave a contented sigh. She could rest now.

"Good morning, pups," said Aspen.

The light coming in through the den entrance disappeared as she came in. Now three weeks old, Lupé and her two brothers, Tarn and Lobo, could see and hear. They were solid little balls that looked more like small bears than wolves. Aspen sniffed each of them and licked their fuzzy gray fur. After a few seconds, she left the pups and went to lie at the den entrance.

The pups had already been exploring the inside of the den, although they were still wobbly. Now they toddled along the tunnel after their mother, pointy tails straight out behind them, with Tarn in the lead. They could hear the other wolves outside. Aspen felt her pups beside her. Teton, watching and waiting, saw a small face appear in the den opening. Tarn's blue eyes blinked rapidly at the bright light. Lupé and Lobo appeared a moment later.

Tails wagging, Teton and the other wolves gathered around the three new pack members. For the pups, it was a little scary—all those noses sniffing and tongues licking. Lobo was rolled right over! But Aspen was there, so it was all right. The pack was excited. These were their pups, too, and they would all take care of them.

Lupé and her brothers stayed close to the den at first. It was a big world and they were still very small wolves. They suckled often and took lots of naps. They got to know the other wolves. Sage and Lily, both females, were Aspen and Teton's pups from the year before, and Sinter, a male, had been born the year before that.

"Ouch!" yelped Lupé. "Your teeth are sharp!" Tarn let go of her muzzle. Lobo watched to see what would happen next.

"Come here, Lupé," Teton called. Tarn and Lobo followed their sister. They didn't want to miss out on anything.

"Play like that is part of finding your place in the pack," Teton told the little wolf when she was sitting by his side. "You have to work out who is the leader among you—who is the most dominant."

"Who is the leader of our pack?" Lupé asked.

"Your mother and I lead the pack together," Teton answered. "She is more dominant than Sage and Lily, and I am more dominant than Sinter. Sage, Lily, and Sinter have their own order of importance among themselves. Sometimes it changes."

"Do all animals live in packs?" wondered Lupé.

"No," replied Teton. "I don't know of any others around here. Wolves are special, and we can do things by working together that a single wolf couldn't do. Hunting is easier when we work as a team. And we take care of pack members who can't take care of themselves."

"Like us!" piped up Tarn.

"Yes, like you," Teton said. "But don't worry, you'll have a chance to do your share for the pack when you are older. Now go play!"

Teton watched as his pups ran off. As usual, Tarn led the way with Lupé hard on his heels. Lobo trotted behind them. Teton got to his feet and slowly stretched. He headed toward the stream for a drink. Stopping for a moment, Teton looked back through the trees. Under the watchful eyes of Sinter and Lily, the pups were romping in the grass—little wolves growing and learning.

"Here they come!" cried Lupé. The pups had waited with Sage while the rest of the pack went hunting. Now the adults were returning, and that meant FOOD!

Lupé and Lobo raced to greet Aspen, wriggling with excitement and licking at her muzzle. Aspen responded by regurgitating, or throwing up, some partly digested elk meat for the pups to eat. As they gulped it down, they saw Tarn doing the same thing with Teton. Sage got her share as well. The other wolves in the pack also fed the pups and their baby-sitter this way.

The pups had begun eating this wolf "baby food" when they were only a month old and still suckling. Now it was mid-June, and Aspen had almost weaned them from her milk. The adult wolves worked hard to get enough meat for themselves and their pups.

The moon had risen on a soft summer night. The pack was hunting while the pups stayed with Sage. Suddenly, a long, lone howl floated through the air. A second voice joined in, and then a third.

"Hey, that's Mom and Dad!" Tarn said.

"Is that Sinter or Lily?" Lobo asked.

"Lily, I think. Sinter's voice is deeper," Lupé answered. She started to say something else, but another set of wolf voices—*different* voices—came from the west.

"Who's that?" Lobo asked, surprised.

"That's the pack across the valley," Sage told them. "There are four or five packs in this area now, but it wasn't long ago that there weren't any wolves here at all."

"Why not?" asked Lupé. "This is a perfect place for wolves."

"Humans killed them all," Sage answered. "They didn't like wolves because some wolves ate cows and sheep. Other people didn't like wolves because wolves ate elk that the people wanted to hunt."

"But wolves *have* to kill elk or some kind of animal—that's how we live!" Lupé was upset.

"I know. But at least humans seem to be learning that we belong here, too." Sage added, "That's why they brought wolves back here. Your grandparents came from the north, from Canada. People caught them and then let them go down here so that this place would have wolves again."

"I still think it stinks that they killed all the wolves in the first place," Tarn said.

"Well, pups," Sage said, "wolves and people have lived beside each other for thousands of years, and they still don't understand each other very well. I don't know if they ever will, but at least the people here seem to be trying."

When only two weeks old, the pups had tried to join in whenever they heard the adults howl. The morning after they heard the wolves across the valley, Tarn boasted, "I bet I can howl just like Dad and Sinter. Listen! Ow-oo-oo-oo!"

"Whoa, I think you need more practice!" Lupé told him.

"We have to be able to communicate," Aspen told Lupé and her brothers, "in order to work as a pack. Howling is only one way we communicate. You must learn all the ways wolves can tell each other things."

The pups watched how the adult wolves used their faces and bodies to send "up close" messages. It worked for the pups, too. When Lupé faced Lobo with her head down low, her rump up in the air, and her tail wagging, Lobo knew that she wanted to play. When Tarn and Lupé were playing and he rolled onto his back, lying there with his tummy showing, Lupé knew that he was giving up.

"Our paws leave a smell behind on the ground," Lupé said to Sinter one day. "Is that a kind of message, too?"

"Yes," said Sinter. "It tells other wolves that we have been here. Our urine and feces do the same thing. That's why we make scent marks with them at the edges of our territory. Other packs know that's the boundary and usually don't cross it. We do the same thing when we come to their territory edges. That way, we don't waste energy fighting each other."

"Wow," Lupé said. "I thought poop was just poop!"

"*My* feather!" yelped Lobo.

"No, it's *mine!*" growled Tarn.

The two pups tugged at opposite ends of a ragged raven feather. Suddenly, Tarn lost his hold and let go. Lobo tumbled over backward.

"Aha!" cried Lupé. "Now it's *mine!*" Darting between her brothers, she snatched up the feather in her teeth and raced away with it. The pups had been playing all morning in the summer sun. They were eight weeks old now, and were growing like weeds. Lupé weighed a little over 9 kilograms (20 pounds), while Tarn and Lobo were about 2.3 kilograms (5 pounds) heavier.

The pack had left the den site, which looked very shabby because of the pups' games. The wolves looked for a rendezvous [RON-day-voo] site, where the pups could stay while the adults hunted. Teton found a sunny, grassy area bordered by trees. Not far away, a creek flowed through a small gully. While the rest of the pack hunted, the pups played here with a baby-sitter, usually Lily or Sage. Sometimes the hunters were away for two or three days at a time before returning with food.

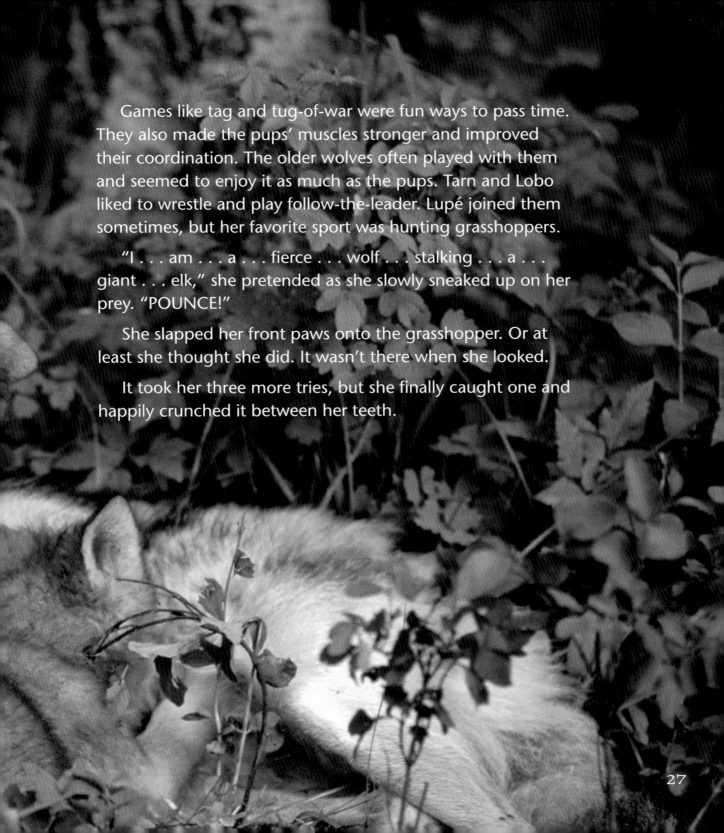

Games like tag and tug-of-war were fun ways to pass time. They also made the pups' muscles stronger and improved their coordination. The older wolves often played with them and seemed to enjoy it as much as the pups. Tarn and Lobo liked to wrestle and play follow-the-leader. Lupé joined them sometimes, but her favorite sport was hunting grasshoppers.

"I . . . am . . . a . . . fierce . . . wolf . . . stalking . . . a . . . giant . . . elk," she pretended as she slowly sneaked up on her prey. "POUNCE!"

She slapped her front paws onto the grasshopper. Or at least she thought she did. It wasn't there when she looked.

It took her three more tries, but she finally caught one and happily crunched it between her teeth.

"What's that, Mom?" Lupé asked. She had spotted a flash of black and white on the edge of a clearing. The pups were trotting along with the pack on short trips now. And there were so many things to see and smell and learn!

"Those are magpies, Lupé," Aspen answered. "There's a bison carcass over there and they must be picking away at it."

"Did you kill that bison? Why don't we go eat some of it, too?" Lupé wondered.

"That was an old bull," Aspen said. "He fought with other males over some cows and was hurt pretty badly. He finally died. We found the carcass when it was fresh and ate some of the meat, but there isn't much left now. The coyotes, ravens, and magpies have done a good job of cleaning it up."

"Do they clean up the animals that you kill, too?" Lupé wanted to know.

"Yes. We eat as much as we can from the carcass and then leave the rest for them." Aspen looked at Lupé. "You know, we can't count on always finding prey, so we eat a lot when we have the chance. When your father is very hungry, he can gobble up a pile of meat that weighs as much as you."

"Wow!" exclaimed Lupé. "Does everybody eat that much?"

"Teton and I eat until we are full," answered Aspen, "and then the others take their turn. If it's a big carcass, we might stay near it for several meals. Grizzly bears and mountain lions sometimes try to take the meat for themselves."

"You know, Lupé, you'll see all this for yourself soon. You're almost old enough now to come to the kill to eat instead of waiting for us to bring you food."

"Really? Wait until I tell Tarn and Lobo!" Lupé dashed off to her brothers with the news.

"Hey, what's all that splashing?" The pups darted out of the brush onto the shore of the lake.

A flock of trumpeter swans churned the water as they took wing. And then another animal caught the pup's attention.

"Look! What is that thing, Lily?" called Lobo.

"Pups!" Lily barked sharply. They ran to her instantly, all thoughts of the animal in the lake forgotten. "You should never go running out into the open like that without looking around first! You don't know what might be out there and you could get hurt," she scolded them. "You're old enough to know better."

"Lily," Lupé said quietly, "what is the animal swimming in the lake? Look, there it is!"

"That's a river otter. They are hunters like us and they're very good at catching fish," Lily told the pups. "And they love to play, like we do. Sometimes you'll see a whole family sliding on their tummies down a slippery bank into the water. They are excellent swimmers."

As the wolves watched, the otter climbed onto the bank and looked at them.

"Huge whiskers!" whispered Tarn.

The otter gave what looked like a grin and bobbed its head at them a few times. Then it dived smoothly into the water and disappeared with hardly a ripple.

One day the pack came to an area of black, dead tree trunks. The pups looked around and sniffed at the trees.

"What happened to these trees?" Lupé wondered.

"There was a big fire and they burned," Aspen replied. "But there will be trees here again. In fact, they needed the fire to start growing."

"What do you mean?" Lupé asked. "How could fire make trees grow?"

"When the fire came, it didn't just burn the trees. It burned all the pine cones lying on the forest floor. The cones came from lodgepole pines. Lodgepoles seal their seeds inside their cones.

It takes heat to make the cones open and let the seeds fall out. The fire did that and it cleared away old trees that would keep the young pines from getting enough light."

"Did the new trees start to grow right away?" Lupé wanted to know.

"Not quite. Purple flowers called fireweed soon grew in the burned areas. Now, the baby pine trees are beginning to grow. They'll make a new forest someday," Aspen added. "Fire can be dangerous but it can be helpful, too."

With that, the wolves moved on, leaving the burned hillside and its infant forest behind.

PLOP. Plopplopplop. PLUUUP. Plop.

"Guys, check this out!" Lupé called. She stood near a big steaming puddle of mud. Bubbles were forming on the surface and bursting, making sounds like a boiling pot of oatmeal. She stuck her nose closer, but jumped back when a big bubble popped and splashed her with hot mud.

"It smells funny around here," Tarn said, wrinkling his nose. "And the ground feels warm under my paws."

"There's steam coming out of the ground over here. What is this place, anyway?" Lobo asked.

"People say there is very hot rock deep in the ground underneath us. It heats the water in the ground until it turns into steam. The steam comes up to the top of the ground and escapes here. Sometimes it just comes out slowly and steadily. Other times it makes mudpots, like the one your sister found. Be careful, Lupé—that mud is hot." Sinter said.

"And it doesn't taste very good, either," said Lupé, licking it off her fur.

"Places like this can be dangerous because steam can shoot out of the ground without any warning. People call the steam jets geysers. All the steam and water means the ground isn't always safe to walk on," Sinter cautioned the pups. "But elk and bison come to these places in the winter, so wolves have to know about them."

"Weird," said Tarn, shaking his head. "Very weird."

It was cold, and Lupé could see her breath. She watched as the yellow leaves of the aspen tree shivered in the breeze. Winter wasn't far away.

"Uh-REEEEE-ooh!" The high-pitched bugle of an elk echoed through the valley. The bull elk were gathering herds of cows and mating with them. Some of the bulls fought off young challengers in antler-to-antler shoving matches.

Black bears and grizzly bears had enjoyed a plentiful berry crop. Plump and sleepy, they were getting ready to tuck themselves away in dens for the winter. Some had already settled in.

Snow began falling, and Lupé looked around to see what everyone was doing. The pups had now grown so much that they were nearly as large as their parents. They hunted small animals like rabbits by themselves, but they were still mainly watching the elk hunts, trying to learn the right things to do. In another month or so, they would be hunting with the pack.

Lupé, Tarn, and Lobo would depend on the others to feed them this winter, but they would be learning all the time. And then spring would come again, bringing a new batch of pups for them to watch over, care for, and teach.

Teton lifted his head and began to howl. Aspen joined him, and then the others raised their voices, too. The wind carried the music they made out over the land.

They were a family, they were a pack—they were wolves.

Here is more information about Yellowstone National Park and many of the wild animals mentioned in this book.

YELLOWSTONE NATIONAL PARK

➤ The park covers almost 9,000 square kilometers (3,500 square miles) and is home to the wildlife mentioned in the story, as well as bald eagles, bighorn sheep, moose, and lynx.

➤ Hydrothermal (hot water) features include the famous geyser named "Old Faithful."

➤ Almost three million people visit the park each year to see the animals and the landscape.

WOLVES

➤ Wolves once lived across nearly all of Eurasia and North America. Today, there are three main areas with large wolf populations. Alaska has about 6,000 wolves, Canada has 40,000 to 60,000, and Russia has 40,000 to 60,000. Other places contain only small, scattered groups.

➤ Wolves were reintroduced to Yellowstone in 1995. By 2003, 148 wolves in 14 packs were living inside the park, with more on the lands nearby. Hunting by humans and loss of habitat were, and are, the main threats to wolves.

➤ The wolf family in this story ate elk, which is the main food of Yellowstone wolves, but wolves eat a wide variety of things, depending on what is available where they live. A few of the other foods they eat are deer, beaver, salmon, birds and their eggs, moose, lemmings, voles, rabbits, hares, and caribou. Wolves also feed on carcasses they find.

➤ Wolf packs usually include breeding adults and some of their offspring. An average-sized litter consists of four to six pups. Most wolf pups leave their home pack when they are one to two years old, to join another pack or form a new one 50 to 100 kilometers (30 to 60 miles) from their birthplace.

➤ Lupé's name comes from the scientific name for the wolf: *Canis lupus* (KAY-nis LOO-pus). Lobo means "wolf" in Spanish. Tarn is another name for a small mountain lake. Aspen is a kind of tree that grows in Yellowstone National Park and elsewhere in the Rocky Mountains. Teton is the name of a mountain range south of Yellowstone. Sage is a plant that grows throughout western North America. Sinter is a deposit of silica, the same stuff sand is made of, left behind by hot water from underground. Lily is named for the glacier lilies that grow in the park.

TRUMPETER SWANS

➤ Trumpeter swans are North America's largest wild fowl, weighing an average of 10 to 12 kilograms (22 to 26 pounds). They were almost wiped out by over-hunting and habitat destruction early in the twentieth century. But today about 20,000 trumpeters live in North America and between 2,000 and 4,000 winter in the Yellowstone region.

RIVER OTTER

➢ A sleek relative of the weasel, the river otter stays warm in water thanks to its thick fur. When it dives, the otter's nose and ears close. Webbed feet make it a strong swimmer.

➢ River otters are about 0.9 to 1.3 meters (3 to 4 feet) long and weigh 5 to 12 kilograms (10 to 27 pounds).

BISON

➢ More than 2,000 bison live in Yellowstone.

➢ They are the largest mammals in the park: a full-grown bull can weigh more than 800 kilograms (1,800 pounds) and stand 1.8 meters (6 feet) tall at the shoulder.

ELK

➢ More than 30,000 elk spend their summers in Yellowstone and about 20,000 winter there.

➢ Each year, bull elk grow new antlers, which can weigh more than 13 kilograms (30 pounds).

➢ During mating season, bulls collect 20 to 30 cows into a group called a harem. Mating season usually ends by November, and calves are born the following spring, in late May or early June.

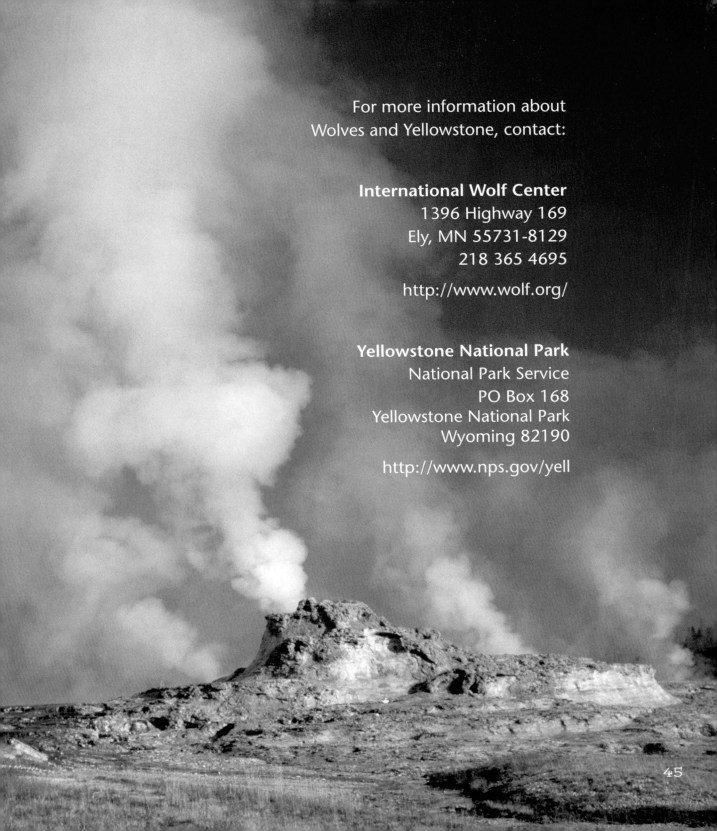

For more information about
Wolves and Yellowstone, contact:

International Wolf Center
1396 Highway 169
Ely, MN 55731-8129
218 365 4695

http://www.wolf.org/

Yellowstone National Park
National Park Service
PO Box 168
Yellowstone National Park
Wyoming 82190

http://www.nps.gov/yell

INDEX

Page numbers in bold refer to pages which contain photographs

Edited by Elizabeth McLean · Proofread by Ian Whitelaw
Cover and interior design by Robert A. Yerks/visualanguage llc.
Printed and bound in Canada

Library and Archives Canada Cataloguing in Publication

Grambo, Rebecca, 1963-
    Lupé: a wolf pup's first year / by Rebecca Grambo;
    photographs by Daniel J. Cox.

(Wild beginnings; 2)
Includes index.
ISBN 1-55285-611-9

1. Wolves—Infancy—Juvenile literature. I. Cox, Daniel J., 1960-
II. Title. III. Series.

QL737.C22G724 2004   j599.773'139   C2004-905000-1

The publisher acknowledges the support of the Canada Council for the Arts and the Cultural Services Branch of the Government of British Columbia for our publishing program.
We acknowledge the financial support of the Government of Canada through the Book Publishing Industry Development Program for our publishing activities.